Nzingha and Being Kind

Story by
Enomwoyi Damali

Art by
George Kelvin Ezechukwu

Nzingha and Being Kind

First Printed in the United Kingdom 2020

Published by Conscious Dreams Publishing
www.consciousdreamspublishing.com

Illustrated by George Kelvin Ezechukwu

Edited by Daniella Blechner

ISBN: 978-1-913674-12-0

DEDICATION

This book is dedicated to everyone who, through their thoughts, words and actions, spreads kindness throughout our world.

ACKNOWLEDGEMENTS

With love always to my husband, Baruti, my four children, and my grand-daughter for their support, encouragement, and confidence in me and my work. Thank you!

And many thanks to the Conscious Dreams Publishing team:
Daniella Blechner, Editor and Publisher;
Oksana Kosovan, Typesetter and George Kelvin, Illustrator,
for helping to turn my idea into this book.

Being Kind

'Good morning Amber Class,' said Mrs Adisa.

'Good morning Mrs Adisa. Good morning everyone,' said the children in Amber Class.

'This week we are learning about being kind. What does being kind mean to you?'

Lots of hands went up, but no one shouted out because when you were in Mrs Adisa's class, you did not shout out. You put up your hand and waited your turn.

'What do you think Kayden?' she asked.

'It's like when my Dad buys me new trainers!' laughed Kayden waving his foot in the air.

'That's not being kind,' said Andrew, 'that's just because you're lucky!'

'So what do you think being kind is Andrew?' asked Mrs Adisa.

'It's when you're kind to someone,' replied Andrew

'And give me an example of being kind to someone?'

'Maybe asking someone to be on your team.'

'Or sharing your crisps with someone,' suggested Stacey.

'Or … passing the ball to someone instead of keeping it all time!' said Andrew in a jokey way.

'What about telling someone that they look gooood?!' said Kayden pointing at himself.

'What about you Nzingha? What do you think?' asked Mrs Adisa.

Nzingha thought for a moment and then she said, 'Maybe kindness is doing anything that makes another person feel happy.'

'That's interesting,' said Mrs Adisa. 'So there must be hundreds and thousands of different ways to be kind.'

'May be even millions and zillions!' laughed Kayden.

'That's a lot of kindness, isn't it?! It would be hard to do millions and zillions of kind things every day, but what about at least five kind things every day?' suggested Mrs Adisa.

'But Mrs Adisa, what if you're kind to someone and they're horrible to you?' asked Rebecca.

'Yeah, like I passed the ball to Kayden and he didn't pass it back so then I couldn't shoot,' complained Andrew.

'And I lent my sister headphones and she wouldn't let me borrow her new top,' moaned Stacey.

'Yes, it's hard when you think you've been kind to someone and maybe they don't return the kindness back to you.'

'My mum says people should be kind just because,' said Nzingha.

'Just because what?' asked Andrew.

'Just because,' repeated Nzingha.

'I like your mum's idea,' said Mrs Adisa, 'It is good to be kind just because ... it is good to be kind.'

The children in Amber Class thought about this.

'And maybe if you are kind you are teaching someone else to be kind too,' added Mrs Adisa.

Amber Class thought about this too.

Being Kind

'So,' said Mrs Adisa, 'Think of five kind things that you will try to do today. You can draw, or write, or cut things out to show your work.'

'Can we make up a play?' asked Kayden.

'Or a song?' asked Stacey.

'Yes you can,' said Mrs Adisa, 'and of course you'll remember our Two Golden Rules.'

'Respect each other and respect school property,' Amber Class said together.

Amber Class were excited as they went off to their tables. They did not rush, of course, because when you were in Mrs Adisa's class, you did not rush anywhere. You waited until Mrs Adisa said the name of your group and then you walked quietly and sensibly to your table.

Mrs Adisa called each group in turn – Mandarin, Gaelic, Creole and Swahili, and the children walked to their tables and started their work.

Mandarin group talked about kindness and wrote a Kindness Acrostic poem together.

Gaelic group talked about kindness. They cut out letters from a magazine and glued them in a pattern to make the word 'kindness' on their paper.

Creole Group talked about kindness. They drew a comic strip with five different kindness pictures.

Swahili group with Nzingha, Kayden, Stacey, Rebecca and Andrew talked about kindness. They made up a song.

Kindness, kindness, it's a gift to give away

Kindness, kindness, it's a gift to share all-day

There's so much we can do

There's so much we can say

We won't run out of kindness anyway

So...

Smile, and share, and hug, and play together, and give, and say hello, and ask 'how are you?', and help, and say something nice, and ... pass the ball!

Amber Class enjoyed working together. When they finished, they shared their work with each other.

'Well done for working together Amber Class. And, thank you for sharing all your wonderful ideas about kindness. At playtime, see if you can do at least one of the kind things you've been talking about.'

Amber Class stood up and, as the children walked out, quietly and sensibly, of course, they said one kind thing they would try to do at playtime.

'I'm going to find someone who's on their own and ask them if they want to play with me,' said Stacey.'

'I'm going to help the younger children if they get stuck on the climbing frame,' said Rebecca.

'I'm going to say hello to the new girl in Year 1,' said Nzingha.

"I'm going to smile at the new girl in Year 1," said Xiaolin.

'I'm going to pass the ball to Kayden,' said Andrew.

'And I'm going to pass it back!' said Kayden.

BEING KIND ACROSTIC

Write a word or a sentence starting with each letter about Being Kind

K _____

I _____

N _____

D _____

N _____

E _____

S _____

S _____

ABOUT THE AUTHOR

Enomwoyi is passionate about helping children develop into the very best that they can be. She has worked as an Educational Psychologist for 30 years (a busy and very satisfying job!) and in her spare time loves writing children's stories about topics that are so important for their development.

Coming soon, other stories about Nzingha and her friends in Amber Class:

- Nzingha and Sorting Thing Out (how to manage angry feelings)

- Nzingha and Feeling Confident

- Nzingha and Making Friends

- Nzingha and Feeling Good

- Nzingha and Celebrating Culture

... and many more!

Conscious Dreams

PUBLISHING

Be the author of your own destiny

Find out about our authors, events, services
and how you too can get your book journey started.

 Conscious Dreams Publishing

 @DreamsConscious

 @consciousdreamspublishing

 Daniella Blechner

 www.consciousdreamspublishing.com

 info@consciousdreamspublishing.com

Let's connect